CLEVER TRICK NUMBER ONE

The Enormous Crocodile crept over to a place where there were a lot of coconut trees. He knew that children often came here looking for coconuts.

He took all the fallen branches and held them between his teeth. He grasped the coconuts in his front paws. Then he stood straight up in the air, balancing himself on his tail.

He now looked exactly like a small coconut tree.

Just then, two children came along.

"Oh look!" cried Toto. "That tree over there is much smaller than the others! And it's full of coconuts! I think I could climb that one quite easily."

The Enormous Crocodile licked his lips. . . .

Bantam Skylark Books by Roald Dahl
Ask your bookseller for the books you have missed

THE
ENORMOUS
CROCODILE

ROALD DAHL

Pictures by Quentin Blake

BANTAM BOOKS
NEW YORK • TORONTO • LONDON • SYDNEY • AUCKLAND

To Sophie

*This edition contains the complete text
of the original hardcover edition.*
NOT ONE WORD HAS BEEN OMITTED.

RL 2, 007–009

THE ENORMOUS CROCODILE
*A Bantam Book / published by arrangement with
Alfred A. Knopf, Inc.*

PRINTING HISTORY

Alfred A. Knopf edition published December 1977

Bantam Skylark edition / April 1984
2nd printing . . . December 1985
3rd printing . . . March 1987
4th printing . . . February 1988

*Skylark Books is a registered trademark of Bantam Books,
a division of Bantam Doubleday Dell Publishing Group, Inc.
Registered in U.S. Patent and Trademark Office and elsewhere.*

ISBN 0-553-15243-2

Published simultaneously in the United States and Canada

---

*Bantam Books are published by Bantam Books, a division
of Bantam Doubleday Dell Publishing Group, Inc. Its
trademark, consisting of the words "Bantam Books" and the
portrayal of a rooster, is Registered in U.S. Patent and
Trademark Office and in other countries. Marca Registrada.
Bantam Books, 666 Fifth Avenue, New York, New York 10103.*

PRINTED IN THE UNITED STATES OF AMERICA

BM   13 12 11 10 9 8 7 6 5

In the biggest brownest muddiest river in Africa, two crocodiles lay with their heads just above the water. One of the crocodiles was enormous. The other was not so big.

"Do you know what I would like for my lunch today?" the Enormous Crocodile asked.

"No," the Notsobig One said. "What?"

The Enormous Crocodile grinned, showing hundreds of sharp white teeth. "For my lunch today," he said, "I would like a nice juicy little child."

"I never eat children," the Notsobig One said. "Only fish."

"Ho, ho, ho!" cried the Enormous Crocodile. "I'll bet if you saw a fat juicy little child paddling in the water over there at this very moment, you'd gulp him up in one gollop!"

"No, I wouldn't," the Notsobig One said. "Children are too tough and chewy. They are tough and chewy and nasty and bitter."

"*Tough* and *chewy*!" cried the Enormous Crocodile. "*Nasty* and *bitter*! What awful tommy-rot you talk! They are juicy and yummy!"

"They taste so bitter," the Notsobig One said, "you have to cover them with sugar before you can eat them."

"Children are bigger than fish," said the Enormous Crocodile. "You get bigger helpings."

"You are greedy," the Notsobig One said. "You're the greediest croc in the whole river."

"I'm the bravest croc in the whole river," said the Enormous Crocodile. "I'm the only one who dares to leave the water and go through the jungle to the town to look for little children to eat."

"You've only done that once," snorted the Notsobig One. "And what happened then? They all saw you coming and ran away."

"Ah, but today when I go, they won't see me at all," said the Enormous Crocodile.

"Of course they'll see you," the Notsobig One said. "You're so enormous and ugly, they'll see you from miles away."

The Enormous Crocodile grinned again, and his terrible sharp teeth sparkled like knives in the sun. "Nobody will see me," he said, "because this time I've thought up secret plans and clever tricks."

"*Clever tricks?*" cried the Notsobig One. "You've never done anything clever in your life! You're the stupidest croc in the whole river!"

"I'm the cleverest croc in the whole river," the Enormous Crocodile answered. "For my lunch today I shall feast upon a fat juicy little child while you lie here in the river feeling hungry. Goodbye."

The Enormous Crocodile swam to the side of the river, and crawled out of the water.

A gigantic creature was standing in the slimy oozy mud on the riverbank. It was Humpy-Rumpy the Hippopotamus.

"Hello, hello," said Humpy-Rumpy. "Where on earth are you off to at this time of day?"

"I have secret plans and clever tricks," said the Crocodile.

"Oh dear," said Humpy-Rumpy. "I'll bet you're going to do something horrid."

The Enormous Crocodile grinned at Humpy-Rumpy and said:

> *"I'm going to fill my hungry empty tummy*
> *With something yummy yummy yummy*
> *   yummy!"*

"What's so yummy?" asked Humpy-Rumpy.

"Try to guess," said the Crocodile. "It's something that walks on two legs."

"You don't mean . . ." said Humpy-Rumpy. "You don't *really* mean you're going to eat a little child?"

"Of course I am," said the Crocodile.

"Oh, you horrid greedy grumptious brute!" cried Humpy-Rumpy. "I hope you get caught and cooked and turned into crocodile soup!"

The Enormous Crocodile laughed out loud at Humpy-Rumpy. Then he waddled off into the jungle.

Inside the jungle, he met Trunky the Elephant. Trunky was nibbling leaves from the top of a tall tree, and he didn't notice the Crocodile at first. So the Crocodile bit him on the leg.

"Ow!" said Trunky in his big deep voice. "Who did that? Oh, it's you, is it, you beastly Crocodile. Why don't you go back to the big brown muddy river where you belong?"

"I have secret plans and clever tricks," said the Crocodile.

"You mean you've got *nasty* plans and *nasty* tricks," said Trunky. "You've never done a nice thing in your life."

The Enormous Crocodile grinned up at Trunky and said:

"I'm off to find a yummy child for lunch.
Keep listening and you'll hear the bones go
crunch!"

"Oh, you wicked beastly beast!" cried Trunky. "Oh, you foul and filthy fiend! I hope you get squashed and squished and squizzled and boiled up into crocodile stew!"

The Enormous Crocodile laughed out loud and disappeared into the thick thick jungle.

A bit farther on, he met Muggle-Wump the Monkey. Muggle-Wump was sitting in a tree, eating nuts.

"Hello, Crocky," said Muggle-Wump. "What are you up to now?"

"I have secret plans and clever tricks," said the Crocodile.

"Would you like some nuts?" asked Muggle-Wump.

"I have better things to eat than nuts," sniffed the Crocodile.

"I didn't think there *was* anything better than nuts," said Muggle-Wump.

"Ah-ha," said the Enormous Crocodile,

> *"The sort of things that I am going to eat*
> *Have fingers, toe-nails, arms and legs and*
> *   feet!"*

Muggle-Wump went pale and began to shake all over. "You aren't really going to gobble up a little child, are you?" he said.

"Of course I am," said the Crocodile. "Clothes and all. They taste better with the clothes on."

"Oh, you horrid hoggish croc!" cried Muggle-Wump. "You slimy creepy creature! I hope the buttons and buckles all stick in your throat and choke you to death!"

The Crocodile grinned up at Muggle-Wump and said, "I eat monkeys, too." And quick as a flash, with one bite of his huge jaws, he bit through the tree that Muggle-Wump was sitting in, and down it came. But just in time, Muggle-Wump jumped into the next tree and swung away through the branches.

A bit farther on, the Enormous Crocodile met the Roly-Poly Bird. The Roly-Poly Bird was building a nest in an orange tree.

"Hello there, Enormous Crocodile!" sang the Roly-Poly Bird. "We don't often see you up here in the jungle."

"Ah," said the Crocodile. "I have secret plans and clever tricks."

"I hope it's not something nasty," sang the Roly-Poly Bird.

"*Nasty!*" cried the Crocodile. "Of course it's not nasty! It's delicious!

"It's luscious, it's super,
It's mushious, it's duper,
It's better than rotten old fish.
You mash it and munch it,
You chew it and crunch it!
It's lovely to hear it go squish!"

"It must be berries," sang the Roly-Poly Bird. "Berries are my favorite food in the world. Is it raspberries, perhaps? Or could it be strawberries?"

The Enormous Crocodile laughed so much his teeth rattled together like pennies in a piggy bank. "Crocodiles don't eat berries," he said. "We eat little boys and girls. And sometimes we eat Roly-Poly Birds, as well." Very quickly, the Crocodile reached up and snapped his jaws at the Roly-Poly Bird. He just missed the Bird, but he managed to catch hold of the long beautiful feathers in its tail. The Roly-Poly Bird gave a shriek of terror and shot straight up into the air, leaving its tail feathers behind in the Enormous Crocodile's mouth.

At last, the Enormous Crocodile came out of the other side of the jungle into the sunshine. He could see the town not far away.

"Ho-ho!" he said, talking aloud to himself. "Ha-ha! That walk through the jungle has made me hungrier than ever. One child isn't going to be nearly enough for me today. I won't be full up until I've eaten at least three juicy little children!"

He started to creep forward toward the town.

The Enormous Crocodile crept over to a place where there were a lot of coconut trees.

He knew that children from the town often came here looking for coconuts. The trees were too tall for them to climb, but there were always some coconuts on the ground that had fallen down.

The Enormous Crocodile quickly collected all the coconuts that were lying on the ground. He also gathered together several fallen branches.

"Now for Clever Trick Number One!" he whispered to himself. "It won't be long before I am eating the first part of my lunch!"

He took all the coconut branches and held them between his teeth.

He grasped the coconuts in his front paws. Then he
stood straight up in the air, balancing himself on his
tail.

He had arranged the branches and the coconuts so
cleverly that he now looked exactly like a small coconut tree standing among all the big.coconut trees.

Soon, two children came along. They were brother
and sister. The boy was called Toto. His sister was

called Mary. They walked around looking for fallen coconuts, but they couldn't find any because the Enormous Crocodile had gathered them all up.

"Oh look!" cried Toto. "That tree over there is much smaller than the others! And it's full of coconuts! I think I could climb that one quite easily if you help me up the first part."

Toto and Mary ran toward what they thought was the small coconut tree.

The Enormous Crocodile peered through the branches, watching them as they came closer and closer. He licked his lips. He began to dribble with excitement.

Suddenly there was a tremendous whooshing noise. It was Humpy-Rumpy the Hippopotamus. He came crashing and snorting out of the jungle. His head was down low and he was galloping at a terrific speed.

"Look out, Toto!" shouted Humpy-Rumpy. "Look out, Mary! That's not a coconut tree! It's the Enormous Crocodile and he wants to eat you up!"

There were no children in the playground at that moment. They were all in school.

The Enormous Crocodile found a big log and placed it in the middle of the playground. Then he lay across the log and tucked in his feet so that he looked almost exactly like a seesaw.

When school was over, the children all came running into the playground.

"Oh look!" they cried. "We've got a new seesaw!"

They all crowded around, shouting with excitement.

"I'll go first!"

"I'll get on the other end!"

"I want to go first!"

"So do I! So do I!"

Then, a girl who was older than the others said, "It's rather a funny knobbly sort of a seesaw, isn't it? Do you think it'll be safe to sit on!"

"Of course it will!" the others said. "It looks strong as anything!"

The Enormous Crocodile opened one eye just a tiny bit and watched the children who were crowding around him. Soon, he thought, one of them is going to sit on my head, then I will give a jerk and a snap, and after that it will be *yum yum yum*.

At that moment, there was a flash of brown and something jumped into the playground and hopped up onto the top of the swings.

It was Muggle-Wump the Monkey.

"Run!" Muggle-Wump shouted to the children. "All of you run, run, run! That's not a seesaw! It's the Enormous Crocodile and he wants to eat you up!"

The children screamed and ran for their lives.
Muggle-Wump disappeared back into the jungle,
and the Enormous Crocodile was left all alone in the
playground.

He cursed the Monkey and waddled back into the bushes to hide.

"I am getting hungrier and hungrier!" he said. "I shall have to eat at least four children now before I am full up!"

The Enormous Crocodile crept around the edge of the town, taking great care not to be seen.

He came to a place where they were getting ready to have a fair. There were slides and swings and dodgem-cars and people selling popcorn and cotton candy. There was also a big merry-go-round.

The merry-go-round had marvelous wooden creatures for the children to ride on. There were white horses and lions and tigers and mermaids with fish tails and fearsome dragons with red tongues sticking out of their mouths.

"Now for Clever Trick Number Three," said the Enormous Crocodile, licking his lips.

When no one was looking, he crept up onto the merry-go-round and put himself between a wooden lion and a fearsome dragon. He sat up a bit on his back legs and he kept very still. He looked exactly like a wooden crocodile on the merry-go-round.

Soon all sorts of children came flocking into the fair. Several of them ran toward the merry-go-round. They were very excited.

"I'm going to ride on a dragon!" cried one.

"I'm going on a lovely white horse!" cried another.

"I'm going on a lion!" cried a third one.

And one little girl, whose name was Jill, said, *"I'm going to ride on that funny old wooden crocodile!"*

The Enormous Crocodile kept very still, but he could see the little girl coming toward him. "Yummy-yum-yum," he thought. "I'll gulp her up easily in one gollop."

Suddenly there was a *swish* and a *swoosh* and something came swishing and swooshing out of the sky.

It was the Roly-Poly Bird.

He flew round and round the merry-go-round, singing, "Look out, Jill! Look out! Look out! Don't ride on that crocodile!"

Jill stopped and looked up.

"That's not a wooden crocodile!" sang the Roly-Poly Bird. "It's a real one! It's the Enormous Crocodile from the river and he wants to eat you up!"

Jill turned and ran. So did all the other children. Even the man who was working the merry-go-round jumped off it and ran away as fast as he could.

The Enormous Crocodile cursed the Roly-Poly Bird and waddled back into the bushes to hide.

"I am so hungry now," he said to himself, "I could eat six children before I am full up!"

Just outside the town, there was a pretty little field with trees and bushes all around it. This was called The Picnic Place. There were several wooden tables and long benches, and people were allowed to go there and have a picnic at any time.

The Enormous Crocodile crept over to The Picnic Place. There was no one in sight.

"Now for Clever Trick Number Four!" he whispered to himself.

He picked a lovely bunch of flowers and arranged it on one of the tables.

From the same table, he took away one of the benches and hid it in the bushes.

Then he put himself in the place where the bench had been.

By tucking his head under his chest, and by twisting his tail out of sight, he made himself look very much like a long wooden bench with four legs.

Soon, two boys and two girls came along carrying baskets of food. They were all from one family, and their mother had said they could go out and have a picnic together.

"Which table shall we sit at?" said one.

"Let's take the table with the lovely flowers on it," said another.

The Enormous Crocodile kept as quiet as a mouse. "I shall eat them all," he said to himself. "They will come and sit on my back and I will swizzle my head around quickly, and after that it'll be *squish crunch gollop*."

Suddenly a big deep voice from the jungle shouted, "Stand back children! Stand back! Stand back!"

The children stopped and stared at the place where the voice was coming from.

Then, with a crashing of branches, Trunky the Elephant came rushing out of the jungle.

"That's not a bench you were going to sit on!" he bellowed. "It's the Enormous Crocodile, and he wants to eat you all up!"

Trunky trotted over to the spot where the Enormous Crocodile was standing, and quick as a flash he wrapped his trunk round the Crocodile's tail and hoisted him up into the air.

"Hey! Let me go!" yelled the Enormous Crocodile, who was now dangling upside down. "Let me go! Let me go!"

"No," Trunky said. "I will not let you go. We've all had quite enough of your clever tricks."

Trunky began to swing the Crocodile round and round in the air. At first he swung him slowly. Then he swung him faster . . .

And *faster* . . .
And FASTER . . .

And FASTER STILL . . .
Soon the Enormous Crocodile was just a blurry circle going round and round Trunky's head.

Suddenly, Trunky let go of the Crocodile's tail, and the Crocodile went shooting high up into the sky like a huge green rocket.

Up and up he went . . .

Higher and higher . . .

Faster and faster . . .

He was going so fast and so high that soon the earth
was just a tiny dot miles below.
He whizzed on and on.
He whizzed far into space.
He whizzed past the moon.
He whizzed past stars and planets.
Until at last . . .

BANG

With the most tremendous
the Enormous Crocodile crashed headfirst into the
hot hot sun.
   And he was sizzled up like a sausage!

Roald Dahl is the author of some of the finest and most widely read children's books ever published, including *Charlie and the Chocolate Factory, James and the Giant Peach, Danny the Champion of the World, The Wonderful Story of Henry Sugar,* and *The Twits.* He is also celebrated for his wonderfully wicked short stories for adults. Mr. Dahl was born in Wales and lives in England.

Quentin Blake has illustrated many favorite children's books, among them *George's Marvelous Medicine* and *The Twits* by Roald Dahl, *How Tom Beat Captain Najork and His Hired Sportsmen* by Russell Hoban, and several stories of his own. His witty cartoons have appeared regularly in *Punch* and *Spectator* and he is a frequent contributor to *Cricket* magazine. He teaches illustration at the School of Graphic Design at the Royal College of Art in London.

Shop at home
for quality children's books
and save money, too.

Now you can order books for the whole family from Bantam's latest catalog of hundreds of titles including many fine children's books. *And* this special offer gives you an opportunity to purchase a Bantam book for only 50¢. Here's how:

By ordering any five books at the regular price per order, you can also choose any other single book listed (up to a $5.95 value) for just 50¢. Some restrictions do apply, so for further details send for Bantam's catalog of titles today.